Ten Old Men and a Mouse

Ten Old Men and a Mouse

CARY FAGAN

Illustrated by

GARY CLEMENT

TUNDRA BOOKS

Published in Canada by Tundra Books,
75 Sherbourne Street, Toronto, Ontario M5A 2P9

Published in the United States by Tundra Books of Northern New York,
P.O. Box 1030, Plattsburgh, New York 12901

Library of Congress Control Number: 2006925480

Library and Archives Canada Cataloguing in Publication

Fagan, Cary
        Ten old men and a mouse / Cary Fagan ; illustrated by Gary Clement.

ISBN 978-0-88776-716-6

        I. Mice – Juvenile fiction.   I. Clement, Gary   II. Title.

PS8561.A375T45 2007   jC813'.54   C2006-902069-8

ONTARIO ARTS COUNCIL
CONSEIL DES ARTS DE L'ONTARIO

We acknowledge the financial support of the Government of Canada through the Book Publishing Industry
Development Program (BPIDP) and that of the Government of Ontario through the Ontario Media
Development Corporation's Ontario Book Initiative. We further acknowledge the support of the Canada
Council for the Arts and the Ontario Arts Council for our publishing program.

The illustrations for this book were rendered in watercolor on Arches paper

Design: Terri Nimmo

Printed and bound in China

1 2 3 4 5 6   12 11 10 09 08 07

In memory of my grandfathers,

Max Fagan and Nathan Menkes.

— C.F.

To Gill, Sarah, and Ben

and to the Kiddush Club.

— G.C.

Like every evening, Max arrived at the synagogue first. After Max came Nat. After Nat came Bud. Then Al, Mose, Herm, Lem, Tov, and Gabe. And last, as usual, came Saul.

Nat had glasses as thick as pop bottles. Al walked with a cane. Mose never remembered to put on his belt, so his trousers were always falling down. Gabe constantly hummed. Saul was always late. All of them had aches or pains in one place or another.

The synagogue was not large or fancy. But for a long time, what a bustling place it had been — everyone crowding in for the Sabbath and the High Holidays! Then children grew up and away, families left the old neighborhood, no one came anymore. So what kept the synagogue going? Ten old men. Ten old men who came every morning and every evening to pray. Each day the same.

Except for this day.

The ten old men had just finished their prayers.

"What's that noise?" said Max.

"A rustle," said Nat, peering through his thick glasses.

"A squeak," said Bud.

"It came from the cupboard." Al pointed with his cane. "We have an intruder among the holy books."

"Well? Open the cupboard door, already," said Mose, pulling up his trousers.

Herm opened the door. Sure enough, sitting beside a stack of prayer books was a mouse.

"Shoo!" said Tov. The mouse turned its head to look at them.

"He isn't running away," remarked Gabe.

"We can all see that," said Saul. "Even Nat can see that."

The mouse began to use its paws to clean its whiskers. "He's making the blessing over the washing of hands," Max said.

"Don't be so clever," said Nat. "We need to get a trap."

"Yes, a trap," agreed Al. "With cheese as bait. We can't have a mouse in the synagogue."

"Peanut butter works better," advised Herm.

"I heard chocolate," said Lem.

"There's a trap in the closet," said Tov. "I'll get it."

The mouse scratched behind its ear with one foot. "I get that same itch," said Gabe.

The mouse blinked and closed its eyes. "Sleepy," said Saul. "He needs an evening nap, like me."

"Here's the trap," said Tov. "Max, you set it."

"I'm not good with mechanical things. Give it to Bud."

"What do I look like, the angel of darkness?"

"Never mind," huffed Al. "I'll do it." He used a piece of bagel for bait. Trying to set the trap, he caught his own finger. "Ouch!"

"Look," said Mose. "The mouse is laughing."

"I'll fix him," said Al. He used a pencil to hold down the spring and then push the trap along the cupboard shelf.

Lowering its ears, the mouse squinted at the trap and then at the men.

"Does he have to look at us like that?" asked Herm.

Lem closed the cupboard and then they went home. That night none of them slept well. Of course, old men don't sleep well most of the time. In the morning, Max arrived first, as always. After him came Nat, Bud, and Al. And then Mose, Herm, Lem, Tov, Gabe, and last, as usual, Saul.

Max said, "Well? Who's going to open the cupboard?"

"Al should," said Nat. "He's the one who set the trap."

"But you all agreed."

"I'll do it," said Bud. Slowly he opened the cupboard door. There was the trap — snapped. Only it wasn't the mouse that was caught. It was Al's pencil.

"I wondered where my pencil went," said Al.

The mouse sat at the end of the shelf, squeaking furiously at them.

"He's giving us a piece of his mind," said Mose.

"Wouldn't you?" shrugged Herm.

"Maybe he's hungry." Lem took a handful of sunflower seeds from his pocket and piled them on the cupboard shelf. The mouse sniffed them, delicately picked one up, and ate.

"I guess it won't hurt to have one mouse in the synagogue," said Gabe. "After all, every life is sacred."

"Besides," said Saul, "he's the first new member we've had in thirty-five years."

After that, the ten old men brought the mouse something to eat every day — a little Gouda cheese, a ripe strawberry, a peanut butter cookie. They gave it a dish of fresh water. They even decorated the cupboard to make it homey. Max put up little pictures cut from magazines. Nat made a bed out of a matchbox. Al brought a tiny table from the old dollhouse that his granddaughter didn't play with anymore. A piece of carpet from Tov made a nice rug.

"All in all," said Bud with satisfaction, "it's a snug little place."

The others couldn't help agreeing, especially when they saw the mouse eating breakfast at the table, or tucked cozily into bed.

The ten old men looked forward to seeing the mouse each day. They lingered after their prayers to admire their new friend.

"Look at those ears!" Al said. "You ever see anything so soft?"

"And those eyes!" Mose added. "Bright as pearls."

"And smart?" said Herm. "There isn't a cat or a dog as smart as our mouse."

"You don't think we're spoiling him, do you?" Lem worried. "He does seem to be getting awfully round."

"Does he look spoiled?" asked Tov. "Does he act spoiled?"

"No," Max said. "He's a perfect little mouse."

Just then a peanut hit Gabe in the nose. "Hey, if you don't want it, just say so!"

The mouse put its paws over its eyes.

"That's all right," said Gabe. "No harm done."

One morning the cupboard door was closed.

"Hey, what gives?" said Max.

"You're shy all of a sudden?" asked Nat.

From inside the cupboard, they heard a low squeak.

"Okay, we get the picture," said Bud. "Who knew that a mouse could be such a prima donna."

In the evening, the door was still closed.
"Hey, mouse!" Al called. "I've got a nice slice of apple."

The cupboard door opened . . . an inch. When Al held out the slice of apple, it was snatched away. The cupboard door thumped shut.

"Can you believe it?" said Mose. "Such rude behavior."

"When we've given him everything he could want," said Herm.

"It just goes to show," said Lem. "Once a rodent, always a rodent."

The next day, Nat said, "Check the cupboard."

"I already did," Max said. "Still closed. That's gratitude for you. I wash my hands of that mouse."

Then they heard something. A squeak. Another squeak. A whole series of squeaks.

"What's that?" said Saul. "Could it be?"

The cupboard door swung open. There stood the mouse. The squeaks were coming from the matchbox bed.

"Look," cried Al. "Babies!"

There they were: small, pink, and squirmy, with their eyes
still closed. The mouse climbed onto the bed and snuggled in
to let them nurse.

"Our mouse is a *she*," said Mose, "and a mother to boot!"

"We ought to celebrate," said Lem.

So, the ten old men got out a bottle of peach schnapps.
They drank a toast. They danced in a circle, singing and clapping.

In time the mice grew. They became furry-soft like their mother. They began to wander out of the bed, first exploring the cupboard, and then the rest of the synagogue. Soon, the ten old men had to be careful. Everywhere they stepped, there was a mouse!

"Having one mouse in the synagogue is one thing," said Gabe. "But this is ridiculous."

"He's right," said Saul. "We can't let them stay."

"But what should we do with them?" asked Max.

"Take them to the country," said Nat. "They'll like it."

"Good idea," said Bud. "Only how will we get there?"

"Easy," said Max. "I'll borrow my old school bus."

"I don't know if that's such a good idea," Al, murmured. Just then a mouse ran up his leg, scrambled onto his shoulder, and somersaulted back into the cupboard. "All right," Al said. "Let's do it tomorrow."

Of course, it wasn't easy to catch all those mice, especially not for ten old men. They used a teacup, a net, a spaghetti strainer, a top hat, a coffeepot, and a rubber boot, and finally, they had those mice – and their mother – in an old guitar case with holes in the top.

The ten old men sat down to catch their breath. Finally, Max said, "Time to go."

Max got behind the wheel, turned the ignition, and put
the bus into gear.

"Hold on," he cried. "It's the country or bust!"

"Be careful," said Saul, cradling the guitar case.

"I guess I'm a little rusty after eleven years in retirement."

The bus lurched again, and they were off.

They found a nice spot in the country. A grassy meadow. A little brook. Bushes laden with juicy raspberries. A shade tree with a comfortable hollow at the roots.

"It doesn't get any better than this," Nat said.

"Paradise," Bud agreed.

They gathered around as Saul gently tipped the case. The mice slid out, squeaking in protest. They sniffed the fresh country air. They took a few steps this way and that. One found the raspberry bushes and called the others over. The mother took a bite of plump raspberry and declared it acceptable for her children.

"Country air makes me hungry, too," said Al.

The mother sniffed at the hollow under the tree. She went in, came out, went in again. Then she used her nose to push her little ones inside.

The ten old men looked down at the hollow. "They don't need us anymore," said Mose, hoisting his trousers. They got into the school bus and Max drove them back to the city.

Summer turned to autumn. As always, the ten old men went to the synagogue every morning and every evening. Max would arrive first, then Nat, Bud, and Al. After them would come Mose, Herm, Lem, Tov, and Gabe. Last, as usual, was Saul. Nat got new glasses — a little thicker now. Al still walked with a cane. Mose's trousers still fell down, while Gabe continued to hum. As for Saul, he came later than ever. After prayers, the ten old men would take off their silk shawls. They still lingered awhile, but not as long as they once had.

One day, Herm said, "Well, it'll be winter soon."

"Do you think it's colder in the country?" asked Lem.

"Not in a hollow under a tree," said Tov. "It's warm enough in there."

"I do miss our mouse," said Gabe.

"We all do," said Max.

And then they heard something.

It came from the door.

"What's that?" asked Nat.

"Open the door and find out," said Bud.

Al opened the door. Nobody. They heard a squeak and looked down. There was the mouse.

"So you came back," said Mose.

The mouse looked up at them and twitched her whiskers.

"Don't tell me," said Herm. "Your children grew up and moved away. An old story."

"Come in, already," said Lem. "You're letting in a draft."

And so she did, scurrying over to the cupboard. The ten old men had left it just as before.

"You hungry?" asked Tov. "We've got poppyseed Danish. Fresh."

Gabe gave a pastry to the mouse. She began to eat.

"Don't worry," Saul said. "You'll hear from your kids again. You know when? When they need something."

The ten old men nodded. The mouse nodded, too.

"Welcome home, mouse," they said.